The GRANDEST Gorgonzola

Written By Jonna Thames & Illustrated By Mari T

THiS BOOK BELONGS TO

_____

This book is dedicated to my one true love

CHEESE

Gilly the GORGONZOLA is feeling rather blue.
The SUN shines on and the water sparkles bright.
But Gilly just feels...well, gloomy and grey.

Gilly just wants to lie in bed ALL DAY.
But the GORGONZOLAS send Gilly on an errand
to buy a jar of HONEY from FRANKIE THE FETA.

Gilly grabs a scarf and...

GRUDGINGLY goes on her way.

3

GiLLY thinks that a shortcut through the park might make her feel better.

"HELLO," Gilly hears and turns to see Charlie the Cheddar.

CREATiVE Charlie waves his PAiNTBRUSH-filled hand.

"Why so glum, GiLLY?"

Gilly shrugs. "Just feeling rather blue."
Charlie the Cheddar, CHARiSMATiC as can be, says,

"Cheer up. GiLLY.
     You're the most
          GOLDEN GORGONZOLA
                                   I know!"

GiLLY continues along the path,
passing PARKER THE PARMESAN.
Parker, as PROPER as ever,
stops with a tip of his hat.
"Good day, young GiLLY."

PEPPER THE POODLE perks up with a proud, "Woof, WOOF."
PARKER continues,
"You're looking mighty GRACEFUL today, GiLLY."

GiLLY smiles and says
THANK YOU
     as PARKER walks away.

HARLOWE THE HAVARTi hastily passes by GiLLY.
But as quickly as HARLOWE hustles, she turns around.
"Howdy, GiLLY!" HYSTERiCAL HARLOWE says.

GiLLY giggles at HARLOWE'S
hilariously HUMONGOUS hat!

HARLOWE smiles in return.

"Glad to see
you giddy,
GiLLY!"

And with one last "HA!",
ARLOWE THE HAVARTI heads on her way.

GiLLY'S smile lingers as a MAJESTIC MELODY fills the air.

"It must be MORGAN THE MOZZARELLA!" Gilly says.

Sure enough, as GiLLY turns the corner, there's MAGNIFICENT MORGAN.

MAGICAL music is coming from right outside FRANKIE'S shop!
GILLY can't help but feel GLEEFUL!

MUSICAL MORGAN gives a grin as GILLY walks into the shop...

...and almost crashes into CAMERON THE CAMEMBERT!
CHiPPER CAMERON chirps with excitement.
"GiLLY! It's wonderful to see you! You're GLEAMiNG!"

GiLLY beams. "Thank you, CAMERON!"
GiLLY steps to the side so CAREFREE CAMERON
can continue on!

"Cheerio," CAMERON calls out with
a FiNAL FAREWELL.

FRANKiE THE FETA says hello with a FLOURiSH.
FRANKiE is as FASHiONABLE as ever!
"Can I help you find some honey, Hunny?"

FRANKiE is also FABULOUSLY FUNNY!
"That would BEE nice," GiLLY says back.
"How GALLANTLY GOOFY you are!" FRANKiE
chuckles.

Honey in hand, GiLLY leaves FRANKiE'S shop, only to find BLAKE THE BRiE dancing BEAUTiFULLY to the beat of MORGAN'S mandolin!

BLAKE boldly beckons GiLLY to do a little BOOGiE.

Together they **WiGGLE AND WAGGLE** and do a **JOVIAL JiG.**
GiLLY and **BLAKE** are bursting with laughter!

"You're so **GROOVY, GiLLY,**" **BLAKE THE BRiE** declares
before dancing **A W A Y.**

GiLLY skips along the shore, SMiLiNG all the way.

"Ahoy there, GiLLY!" SKiPPER THE SWiSS squawks from a ship.

"Good day, SKiPPER!" GiLLY sounds out.

SEAFARING **SKIPPER** sails smoothly toward GILLY.

"How are ya, Matey?" **SKIPPER** questions.

"You know what, **SKIPPER**. I'm feeling **GREAT**,"
GILLY THE GORGONZOLA says.

"Even when I'm feeling just a little BLUE,
or even rather GLOOMY AND GREY,
I know that things will be okay

BECAUSE I KNOW I'M...

Stay up to date with our **CHEESY** characters
and get a free set of digital recipe cards at

WWW.THEGRANDESTGORGONZOLA.COM

Prepared for publication by:

Thames Press

Illustrations by Mari T

Cover design by Jonna Thames

Published in the United States of America

www.TheGrandestGorgonzola.com

CPSIA information can be obtained
at www.ICGtesting.com
Printed in the USA
BVHW021204290721
613179BV00009B/1288